Our Diamond

A Tragedy in One Act

by Clint Miller

Baker's Plays
7611 Sunset Blvd.
Los Angeles, CA 90042
bakersplays.com

CAST OF CHARACTERS

Females:
MAGI
RUTH
HANDLESS
JEWELER
JO

Males:
GUARD
THREE ATTENDANT GUARDS (nonspeaking)

SETTING

A blank room with a doorway at the back.
Two black boxes or crates in the foreground.

PRODUCTION INFORMATION

OUR DIAMOND had its premiere performance on March 12, 2007 in Abingdon, VA. The production was Directed by Melanie Lashinsky, Stage Management and Lighting by Amanda Phillips, with Make-up by Katie Nichols. The cast was as follows:

MAGI . . . . Megan Pfefferkorn
RUTH . . . . Emily Swan
JEWELER . . . . Margaret Hollifield
HANDLESS . . . . Olivia Gibian
JO . . . . Hannah Jamison
GUARD . . . . Will Garrison

UNSPEAKING ATTENDANT GUARDS: . . . . Kolton Powers
Stephan Redman
Jayson Brooks

*(**HANDLESS**, **JO**, and **JEWELER** are "surrounding"
MAGI, clapping and cheering. **RUTH** does not partici-
pate but still watches.)*

JO. One more!

HANDLESS. Please!

JEWELER. Yes, one more!

MAGI. Oh, but I don't have enough time.

JEWELER. Time?

MAGI. Yes. Just look at my watch.

JO. But you don't – none of us has a watch.

MAGI. Well what is this, then? Look closer. Closer. Here.

*(**JO** begins pulling a long series of connected scarves from
MAGI's sleeve. When all the scarves are out, **HANDLESS**,
JO, and **JEWELER** clap and/or cheer.)*

RUTH. How did you smuggle those scarves in?

*(**HANDLESS**, **JO**, and **JEWELER** lose their enthusiasm to
silence.)*

JO. I don't believe that is a fitting question.

RUTH. *Why* did you smuggle those scarves in?

JO. Why must you ask these things? Why must you remind
us of our surroundings? She was using all of her art
to make us forget and – and she did a fine job of it. A
fine job indeed, until you did a fine job of ruining it
for all of us.

RUTH. Your eyes were all already open before I opened my
mouth.

MAGI. Yes, their eyes were open yet they did not see the
scarves until I so desired. Now my friends, shall I reveal
one more surprise? These surroundings? These surroundings of which you speak? We are standing on a
stage – and there – there is a crowd intently watching.
Move, move, move – there – do you see them?

(They stare at the audience)

RUTH. That is just a wall!

MAGI. And this is just a sleeve, until…*(revealing quite a large diamond)*

HANDLESS. It's –

JEWELER. A diamond!

JO. What a diamond!

RUTH. What? But, where – How?

(Enter GUARD *with attendant guards.* MAGI *hides the diamond.)*

GUARD. Inspection time. Quick. Quick. Ok. Ok. You're getting thinner. *(removing hat/helmet to dust it)* You should eat something – before we burn every last one of your calories in that gigantic furnace outside. What? You don't feel like laughing anymore? I just heard all of your cheering and ruckus and laughter from outside. I thought you would like a reminder of the real joke. What? You don't get it? Perhaps you need some laughing gas? *(replacing hat/helmet)* In good time, the gas will come for you, you wretched dirty Jews. Now keep quiet.

(Exit GUARD *with attendant guards.)*

MAGI. Where was I? Yes, of course. This is a stage. And that? That was the villain of our little play. The audience, I'm sure, could understand as much, immediately, on account of his terrible haircut.

*(*HANDLESS, JO, *and* JEWELER *laugh.)*

JO. I'm glad our "audience" wasn't close enough to smell him!

JEWELER. Sauerkraut gone bad!

HANDLESS. And the way he walks! *(miming)*

MAGI. *(to the audience)* Oh yes, he is our villain, ladies and gentlemen. No doubt about that.

RUTH. Stop it! Stop this nonsense! *You are talking to a wall for God's sake!* Don't you realize where we are? Do you not know what fate awaits us? My family has already met that fate – my two sons and daughter, my husband, sisters, brother, father, mother – and – and soon we all will join them. Why must you play these stupid games, staring at this wall when only death is staring back at us?

(silence)

JEWELER. What about the diamond?

HANDLESS. The diamond!

JO. Yes! Yes! Let us see it again!

ALL THREE. Please!

MAGI. The guards, they searched me diligently but –*(to* **RUTH***)* could you move just a bit to the left, please? You are blocking their view. *(to the audience)* Yes, the guards, they searched me thoroughly – every inch of me they searched – but many things they did not discover. *(displaying the diamond)* Yes, my father and my mother – who are dead now too, by the way – poor father and mother always discouraged my love of this art. "But mamma, papa!" I would cry, "I shall be the best magician in all of Germany!" "But how, my daughter," they would say to me with loving worry, "how will you find any success in such a lowly hobby? Find a wealthy husband to love instead. Stop wasting your life perfecting useless slight-of-hand trickery and find a rich husband." But what would they say – what would they say if they could only know that through my lowly hobby, through my slight-of-hand trickery, I am now the richest woman in all of Auschwitz?

RUTH. They would say you've gone crazy – talking to a wall. What good will that diamond do us here?

JO. You could bribe the guard to free us!

RUTH. Ha! As soon as he finds out about that diamond he will only take it – just as he took all of our other possessions.

MAGI. He took two of my molars for the golden fillings. I could not hide my teeth when he pried my mouth open. But this? This? *(turning around and hiding the* *diamond in her clothing)* He will never find our diamond!

RUTH. How could he not find it? It is only up your sleeve there.

MAGI. Search me.

*(**RUTH** searches.)*

HANDLESS. Why do you call it *our* diamond?

MAGI. As soon as the guard finds out about this diamond, he will consider it his property. Why should he have such a privilege? And why shouldn't you? Why shouldn't all of you? You all now know about this diamond. It is yours. It is all of ours.

RUTH. I – I – I can't find it. That is – that is unbelievable. I searched all over you.

MAGI. But did you search here?

*(**MAGI** pulls the diamond from **RUTH'S** pocket. **JO, JEWELER,** and **HANDLESS** applaud and/or cheer.)*

RUTH. What? That is impossible!

MAGI. What is impossible is the expression on your face.

RUTH. *(She is smiling but she almost doesn't know it. She feels her face, slowly.)* I – I haven't smiled for – for two years at least. I – I –

*(Enter **GUARD** with attendant guards. **MAGI** conceals the diamond.)*

GUARD. What was all that clapping? What did I tell you? Come to order. Order, now! You – wipe that stupid smile off your face! *(hitting **RUTH**)* What do you have to be happy about? Look around. You know where you are.

RUTH. Yes. I know exactly where I am. I am on a stage, and – *(to audience)* and something smells like rotten sauerkraut!

*(**GUARD** hits her again, knocking her to the floor.)*

GUARD. Let that be a lesson to all of you. Now keep quiet.

*(Exit **GUARD** with attendant guards.)*

MAGI. That was an exemplary performance! Are you hurt?

RUTH. No. I feel. I feel better than I've felt in a long while. May I…may I touch it?

MAGI. Of course, my dear, you are part owner. *(handing her the diamond)*

RUTH. *(almost crying)* It is the most beautiful thing I have ever seen, ever felt, ever held.

JEWELER. *(moving for the diamond)* Excuse me, but could I take a closer look? I am – at least I was – a jeweler in Berlin, working side by side with my husband in our little shop before…well before all this.

MAGI. *(taking the diamond from* **RUTH** *to keep it from* **JEWELER***)* A jeweler? You have probably seen enough diamonds to fill a lifetime! Diamonds probably bore you by now!

JEWELER. I have never seen a diamond so big. I must take a closer look. *(reaching for it)* Do you realize how much it could be worth?

MAGI. *(pulling away)* It is worth so much that I am afraid that when an expert like yourself finds out the true value you will drop dead of disbelief!

JEWELER. Please just let me hold it for one second. Just a touch at least. It would mean so much to me. Every day, back then, back in Berlin, in my husband's shop, back in my normal life – every day I handled precious jewels and gems and diamonds and thought nothing of it. I saw so many valuable things that they became worthless to me. But now? To touch this diamond –

MAGI. Our diamond.

RUTH. Our diamond.

JO AND HANDLESS. Our diamond.

JEWELER. To touch our diamond I could feel – I could know – I could feel real value for the first time, almost. I could –

MAGI. *(handing the diamond to* **JEWELER***)* Hold it carefully. Please understand the…the delicacy involved I beg you.

JEWELER. *(beginning to cry)* I don't – I don't – I don't know what to say. It is a – it is a –

MAGI. Please –

JEWELER. It is the most valuable thing I have ever touched.

JO. May I hold it too?

HANDLESS. And me? And me, as well?

MAGI. Pass around our diamond! Let everyone get their fill of feeling it.

OTHERS. *(whispering as they receive the diamond in turn)* Marvelous, fantastic, breathtaking, etc…

RUTH. *(taking the diamond)* Oh – let's show it to our audience, shall we? *(to the audience)* Look! Look at our diamond, can you see it? Of course you can see it. It is enormous! How you all must envy us! *(to others)* Think how they must envy us.

JO. Anyone would give their life to be in our shoes now – to touch our diamond and to possess it!

HANDLESS. We are lucky. Truly lucky. Look – oh just look at our beautiful diamond!

MAGI. *(taking the diamond)* All of you who look upon our stage – how you must wish that you were here with us! How you must wish to taste a tiny morsel of our riches!

(Enter **GUARD** *with attendant guards.* **MAGI** *hides the diamond.)*

GUARD. What is this? I've told you to be quiet. Told you many times, but now you all are shouting? Shouting now of riches?

(quiet)

GUARD. I know this silence. This silence buries treasure – I have heard it many times before. *(indicating gun)* Do not make me use my shovel. I will have this treasure. Out with it. *(silence)* Out with it! Hand it over – I know there must be something you are hiding. I can see it on your scheming faces. I can hear it in your hushed breaths. I will kill every last one of you if I have to.

RUTH. Kill us then – you will never have it!

GUARD. There – she admits it! You are hiding something valuable? Do you know the punishment?

HANDLESS. We shall all die soon enough, anyway.

GUARD. I will tear your bodies piece by piece apart until I find it! I will keep you all alive while I am ripping through your flesh so that you may feel the consequences of this foolish hoarding! Hand it over! Hand it over now or you will all die painful deaths and I will pluck your filthy treasure from piles of flesh and blood.

(tense pause)

RUTH. It is –

OTHERS. *(simultaneously)* No! Stop! Don't! etc…

RUTH. Our treasure is a –

OTHERS. *(simultaneously)* No! Stop! Don't! etc…

RUTH. It is a diamond! Yes, a diamond!

GUARD. Where! Give it to me!

RUTH. *(quickly looking at* **MAGI**, *who has it hidden)* It is – It is – It is embedded in my molar – beneath a metal filling. Do you see the filling? Here?

GUARD. Yes I see the metal filling. So the diamond is beneath it?

RUTH. Yes.

GUARD. You see? That wasn't so hard, was it? All that fuss – over a little diamond? Come with me.

(They exit with attendant guards.)

JO. What will they do to her?

MAGI. Oh, they will remove her molar. It is a painful process. *(displaying the diamond)* But what is pain compared to such a diamond? She knows this just as well as we do.

HANDLESS. *(taking the diamond)* I had a diamond ring once. I had – I had a husband. He was killed. Two years ago. The diamond ring he gave me when he asked me for my hand – that diamond ring, when they brought me here, they tried to take it from me and I – of course I fought them. Three guards and I fought them all as if they were the ones who had killed him. And for all I know they might have been. I fought them – oh I fought them bloody black and blue and they could not pull that diamond ring from my finger, from my clenched fist, and I fought them. I fought them. I fought them but it was – it was futile but it was – it was glorious as well. They subdued me after fifteen or twenty minutes – those three guards and two more who came to help them. Yes it truly took five guards to hold me down. Five of the monsters. And I lay there on the bloodied floor lunging and wriggling under their grip and kicking and wailing and, yes, crying too, but I still fought through the tears, as their collective force tightened around me, like a boa constrictor until I had no breath left and I was still – but, but, but my fists – both fists – both fists were still tightly clenched. I was still – I was still fighting and, and no matter how hard they tried, they could not open my fingers to remove my diamond ring.

JO. Why would you struggle so against them when you know that they must win?

HANDLESS. But they did not win! They did not win! This is my trophy. *(holding up arm with missing hand)*

JEWELER. Are you – are you –

JO. Are you joking?

HANDLESS. I am victorious. The ring never left my finger.

JO. But…but they…they chopped off your entire hand and surely then they…they must have taken the ring from your finger then.

HANDLESS. After they removed my hand it was not *my* finger. While I had possession of my finger, the ring never left it. I have beaten the Nazis – listen! Listen well. I have beaten the Nazis and they admitted it when they took my hand from me. The brutal pain – the loss – the bloody suffering – that was my most poignant taste of triumph, and every time I look down upon this missing hand, this hideous lump, my heart swells with pride. For I hold in this hand a victory the Nazis can never steal from me.

(Enter **GUARD** *with attendant guards. They bring* **RUTH** *with them, throwing her toward the others.* **RUTH** *is bleeding from the mouth. Her eyes have been cut out, and blood trickles down her cheeks like tears. Perhaps there is a bloody rag covering her non-existent eyes.)*

GUARD. You tell them what I told you. Tell them every-thing.

(Exit **GUARD** *with attendant guards.* **RUTH** *is on her knees, weeping.)*

JEWELER. What happened?

JO. What have they done to you?

MAGI. Please. Please. Do not cry. They want you to cry. Do not cry. *Please!*

RUTH. Cry? Can I even cry without tears? Without eyes?

MAGI. What have they done?

RUTH. My tooth – they took my molar – they – they did not pull it out. No. They struck me with the butt of a rifle until I spit it to the ground. And then they greed-ily fell upon it, on the bloody floor, fighting among themselves like – like animals. Finally they removed the metal filling to look for the diamond underneath but – but there was no diamond.

JO. But why? Why would you lie to them?

RUTH. What else could I have done? You heard his threats. He would have killed all of you – all of us – that instant had I not distracted him with that lie and now…the lie has bought us these few more minutes with our dia-mond. It cost me just a tooth and these two eyes.

JEWELER. Why would they –

RUTH. He knows that we are hiding something valuable. He knows. He said if I had the audacity to hide a treasure from his sight, he would remove my own sight and –

JO. Sit down – no – do not stand. You've lost too much blood already.

RUTH. He told me to tell you to produce the diamond or –

JO. Sit down – please sit, your body cannot take this!

RUTH. Or he will kill us all and search our corpses until he finds it. *(feeling the "wall" in front of her with her hands outstretched toward the audience)* Oh – what is this? A wall? But – but where is the audience? How can they see us through this? I – I thought – I thought we were standing on a stage but what is this damn wall? *What is this damn wall?*

MAGI. No – don't worry about the wall. No. The audience can see straight through it – I'm sure of it. I'm sure of it. For all the world will someday know of us, and they will view us on this stage through history – straight through this wall – they will see us! They will see us! They are looking at us now! Do you feel them watching? You must feel them watching!

RUTH. I – I – I can't –

MAGI. Feel this. *(handing her the diamond)* Feel our diamond – feel the wealth and joy and beauty that is ours alone and now – now…can you feel them watching you? You must feel them watching!

RUTH. *(very emotionally)* Yes! Yes! I can – I can feel them! Oh I can feel them! I can feel them!

MAGI. *(to the others)* Can you all feel them? Can you?

OTHERS. *(staring out into the audience)* Yes! Yes!

JO. But soon…soon our audience will have to watch our deaths. The guard will surely kill us if –

HANDLESS. If we don't give up the diamond we shall die, and if we do give up the diamond? What do you think will happen then? We all shall die soon enough. *(to the audience)* The Nazis know this just as well as us. But do you know what we will show them? *(to the others)* Do you know what we will we show them? *(this time "them" refers to the audience)*

OTHERS. What?

HANDLESS. We are going to show them the most beautiful victory they have ever seen! Let all of history watch us on this stage! Let all of history know about our diamond!

RUTH. *(stumbling)* This is –

JO. She has lost too much blood!

RUTH. *(holding up the diamond, though nearly falling)* This is –

JO. Hold her – she is falling!

RUTH. This is the greatest day of my entire life.

(She dies. One of them has caught her, and now they all help to lay her down, quietly. **MAGI** *takes the diamond. Enter* **GUARD** *with attendant guards.* **MAGI** *conceals the diamond.)*

GUARD. What? *(poking* **RUTH** *with his boot)* She is dead so soon? You inferior Jews loose some eyes and a tooth and a little blood and it is enough to kill you? *(to one of the attendant guards)* Remove the stinking body. *(to the others)* Do you see that? Do you see that miserable pile of curdled blood and brittle dead bones? She got it easy compared to what I will do to you all. Now, I know you are hiding something. Gold? Gems? Silver? Diamonds, most likely. Something terribly valuable. I can smell it on your foul breath. Whoever presents it to me now shall be spared. *(pause)* What? You place no value in your lives?

(At some point during the previous words, one of the attendant guards has dragged or carried out **RUTH** *'s body.)*

HANDLESS. We place more value in our diamond!

GUARD. *(to* **HANDLESS** *)* You! *(to one of the attendant guards)* Take her away. Kill her, then search her body completely.

(One of the attendant guards exits forcefully with **HAND-LESS,** *who wears a victorious expression.)*

GUARD. Look at you. Look at those faces! I can see that she must not have had the diamond that she spoke of. What a waste. And what purpose does this serve – this silence? This hiding? This hoarding? I will have it. I will have the diamond! I will have it! Save yourselves and hand it over – I'll spare you for it. *(silence)* No? Then you shall die for that diamond – and I will soon have it.

JO. As if our deaths were not already in your plans!

MAGI. As if we feared such trivial things!

GUARD. As if your voices were not shaking!

MAGI. You want the diamond? You want a fortune? You shall never have it.

GUARD. I will find it.

MAGI. I have it with me right now. The greatest treasure in the world – I have it hidden – it is mine and you will never find it.

GUARD. You confess? *(to the last remaining attendant guard)* Seize her.

(The attendant guard does not make it to her before the next line.)

JO. I have it with me, now, as well. And you will never have it.

GUARD. What is this? A second confession? One of you lies. Or both.

JEWELER. I have it too! I have it with me! I have the treasure! It is ours and you will never have it!

GUARD. All of you? All of you? *(pause)* Do not toy with me. *(indicating gun)* I will toy with you.

MAGI. Perhaps you do not understand the nature of our treasure.

GUARD. I will find it!

MAGI. You will only find what you deserve: defeat and humiliation.

GUARD. You wish to force my hand? You wish to force this hand?

*(striking **MAGI**, then seizing her, then speaking to the attendant guard, referring to **JO**)*

Seize her – she was the second to confess. We will search these two – no, first we will kill these two. Then we will search them. *(to* **JEWELER***)* Then I shall return for the third confessor.

JO. *(almost laughing or shrieking as she is seized by the attendant guard)* You will never find the treasure that you seek! It could never be yours.

GUARD: *(struggling with* **MAGI***)* Take her away!

(The attendant guard drags **JO** *from the room, then* **GUARD** *speaks to* **MAGI***, who is still struggling.)*

Stop resisting – you know what must happen now.

MAGI. *(breaking from his grip and hugging* **JEWELER** *in order to sneak the diamond into her pocket)* My friend and fellow actress – I believe this is the closest I will come to a curtain call. I now take my leave of our little play.

*(***GUARD** *tries to pull her off.)*

Goodbye.

GUARD. Get off of her!

MAGI. Good luck.

GUARD. Now! Your death awaits.

MAGI. *(pulling away from* **JEWELER** *and also pulling away from* **GUARD'S** *grip, dusting her clothes, taking one last look at the audience, then at* **JEWELER***.)* Good show.

(She bows to the audience, and then **GUARD** *seizes her again.)*

GUARD. Enough!

(They exit. Spotlight appears on **JEWELER***. She is now all alone on the stage. She pulls the diamond from her pocket where* **MAGI** *hid it. She is almost surprised to find the diamond there.)*

JEWELER. *(to the audience)* Her slight-of-hand, her beautiful art never failed her. Now she will lose her life like some cheap magic trick. Poof and it is gone. The others too. Like a rabbit disappearing into a hat. *(snaps)* Just like that…I – I – I almost can't believe what just occurred. All of them so – so – so suddenly gone and so suddenly dead? But everything about this holocaust was sudden and unexpected. Why should this be any different? This feeling? It leaves you with the taste of disaffected disbelief, such death. Is it really over? Just like that? What is this feeling?

What is death? Everyone must die – but who could ever die as rich as we have been? Yes I have seen a thousand diamonds, gems, and rubies in my former profession. But I have never seen anything as valuable as this. For this has bought us happy deaths. This has made our hearts into impenetrable vaults where we store our most priceless possession. This – this in itself is worthless here. A diamond in the rough? What good are diamonds in Auschwitz? But through this we have found a crystallized meaning – a brief reason for living, and now, yes, a beautiful reason for dying too. Look how gorgeously stunning this reason is. Just look at it! The others – they are picturing it now, no doubt, and whatever the Nazis do to them, whatever awful torture they endure before a bloody death, it all is trivial, overshadowed, overcome through this. Our diamond.

(Spotlight disappears. Enter **GUARD**. *He is weary, rattled, disheveled, covered in blood, and almost crazed from the torture he just inflicted.* **JEWELER** *hides the diamond when he enters.)*

GUARD. Sit down. Sit down.

*(***JEWELER*** and ***GUARD*** *sit upon each crate.)*

It is done. They all are dead and searched and…nothing. So I know you must have the diamond. Soon I shall be rich beyond my dreams. *(almost to himself)* My dreams…but sleep – will sleep come to me? And when it does what will I see? *(to* **JEWELER***)* Your friends – I tortured them terribly before I killed them. They – I tortured them brutally but they – all of them – they died…*smiling!* They – they – they died *happily!* *(pause)* Never will I sleep again without seeing those – those damn unconquerable smiles – *(standing)* THOSE

DAMN UNCONQUEARBLE SMILES but – but *(sitting)* – but it is no matter now for soon I shall be rich. And you? You can give me the diamond now. It makes no difference – I will kill you either way – but it would be much easier for you to just hand it over now.

JEWELER. I will. I have it here.

GUARD. You have it!

JEWELER. But first I must tell you two things.

GUARD. I am rich! I am filthy rich! Go on and say what you must say, you wretched Jew, and hurry up. I am rich!

JEWELER. The first thing I will tell you as a jeweler. The second I will tell you as a Jew.

GUARD. Well go on, then. What does the jeweler have to say?

JEWELER. I have studied diamonds since I was a young girl, ever since I met my late husband. I have learned everything there is to know about diamonds. I have learned to calculate the value to the smallest decimal.

GUARD. Yes? Yes? And what's it worth? A fortune, sure! A fortune, yes?

JEWELER. This diamond has a double value. I saw that from the start. It is worth more than my life or the lives of the others which you just took. It is so valuable to us that we would happily die for it. We would happily endure anything for it. At the same time, however, I have known one other thing from the very start, ever since I first touched the diamond. Ever since I first laid eyes on it I suspected –

GUARD. Yes? Yes?

JEWELER. *(revealing the diamond)* It is a fake. It is an obvious fake. Just look at it. It is a wonder that the others did not realize – and, and perhaps they did. In fact – in fact, I'm sure they did.

GUARD. A…fake?

JEWELER. *(handing him the diamond)* Just look at it! Feel it and you can easily tell. The weight…the density…Just – just look at it. It is an obvious fake.

GUARD. It – it – it – it cannot be. IT CANNOT BE! A fake? A fake? It is! Look at this! A diamond? This? No! It can't be! I was going to be – I was going to have a diamond! I was going to be rich beyond my dreams and now – and now – and now? A fake? A fake!

JEWELER. That is what the jeweler had to tell you.

GUARD. *(trying to regain his composure and to appear calm, yet not exactly succeeding)* What – what does the Jew have to say then? First the jeweler spoke and now the Jew? I will kill you both.

JEWELER. *(standing)* The Jew would like to tell you that to us that fake diamond was worth more than all the world could give us. You know first-hand of this. And that value – that precious value – we have stolen that from you, just as you have stolen everything from us. Yes. Look at the expression on your face. You've been robbed! That is priceless. Invaluable.

GUARD. *(standing, dropping the diamond to the floor)* A Jew tells me this? The Jew tells me this? You are done now? Are you ready for your death?

JEWELER. This Jew would like to tell you one last thing.

GUARD. *(pointing and cocking his gun)* Go ahead.

JEWELER. *(looking directly at the audience)* Do you know that we are right now standing on a stage? Do you know this? Look out there – do you see? Do you see the eyes of History? They have just watched your humiliating defeat, and they have savored it just as much as I. I know you feel them watching too – I see it in your eyes! Yes, we are standing on a stage and all the world has just witnessed a beautifully heated, hardened, crystallized diamond victory. Us Jews? We will have that forever – and you? *(picking up the diamond from the floor and smiling at it)* You have nothing.

(Lights go out. Gunshot is heard.)

Finis

Christ in the Concrete City

By Philip Turner

4m / 2f / bare stage / 1 hour

Revised edition. There have been hundreds of productions of this, one of the most eloquent Christian dramas ever written -- a constant best seller. "The most significant passion play of our time." -- A. Edyvean, His Dramatic World. A powerful drama which sets before us a typical group of people. The actors play both historical characters in the Bible story, and characters from their own lives, passing freely to and from each world. As the playwright states in this revised edition: "I believe it should stand as it was when in rage I wrote it . . . . a young man when he assaulted and was repulsed by the concrete walls of the city of our pseudo-scientific secularism."

Please visit our website **bakersplays.com** for complete descriptions and licensing information

After The Rain King

By Steph DeFerie

Full Length / 4m, 4w, 6 m or f or as many as 22 can be cast / Single set with additions. Glory may be just a little kid but she's in big trouble - when she accidentally opens an old, locked book she finds in an old trunk, a mysterious stranger jumps out! "I am the Rain King, The Lord Of Tears, The Master Of Sorrows, The Commander of the Darkness in your soul! I suck the happiness from your thought and leave only fear and desolation. Destruction is my bread and butter, loss is my meat and drink!" And Glory is the one responsible for releasing him from his prison and setting him free in the world again! Before she can stop him, he kidnaps Pete and disappears back into the book. To rescue Pete, Glory and her friends must follow and soon find themselves jumping from story to story - battling pirates in "Treasure Island", helping young Arthur pull the sword from the stone in "Le Morte D'arthur" facing down bank robbers in "Prairie Rustlers" and even becoming bugs! Can they save Pete, not to mention the rest of the world, from this dangerous monster or will he cast his evil spell over us all. A funny chilling and imaginative play with an exciting climax.

Please visit our website
bakersplays.com
for complete descriptions and licensing
information